D0515651

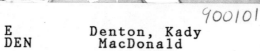

900101

E
DEN     Denton, Kady
        MacDonald

        Dorothy's dream

$12.95

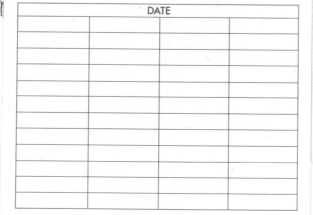

| DATE | | |
|---|---|---|
| | | |
| | | |
| | | |
| | | |
| | | |
| | | |
| | | |
| | | |
| | | |
| | | |
| | | |
| | | |
| | | |
| | | |
| | | |

© THE BAKER & TAYLOR CO.

For children who don't want
to go to sleep

Copyright © 1989 by Kady MacDonald Denton

All rights reserved. No part of this book may be reproduced or
transmitted in any form or by any means, electronic or mechanical,
including photocopying, recording, or by any information storage
and retrieval system, without permission in writing from the Publisher.

Margaret K. McElderry Books
Macmillan Publishing Company
866 Third Avenue
New York, NY 10022

Printed in Italy
First published 1989 by Walker Books Ltd, London
First United States Edition

10  9  8  7  6  5  4  3  2  1

Library of Congress Cataloging-in-Publication Data
Denton, Kady MacDonald.
Dorothy's dream / Kady MacDonald Denton.—1st ed.
p.    cm.
Summary: Dorothy does not like going to sleep because she is
afraid she will miss something, but then one night she discovers the
magic of dreams.
[1. Dreams—Fiction.  2. Sleep—Fiction.  3. Bedtime—Fiction.]
I. Title.
PZ7.D436Do  1989   [E]—dc19    88-28589    CIP    AC
ISBN 0-689-50482-9

# Dorothy's Dream

## Kady MacDonald Denton

*Margaret K. McElderry Books*
NEW YORK

"What will we do with Dorothy?"
asked her mom and dad. "She doesn't
like going to sleep."

"She sings and dances on her bed," said Dorothy's sister.

"She looks at books and draws pictures," said Dorothy's brother.

Upstairs, in her pink-and-white bedroom, Dorothy sang and danced.

"I don't like going to sleep," she said. "I might miss something."

"Tra-la-la," sang Dorothy as she bounced on her bed.

Upstairs,
Dorothy looked
at books.

Downstairs, Dorothy's sister played
her recorder.

Downstairs, Dorothy's
brother called in the cat.

Upstairs, Dorothy drew pictures.
"I don't want to go to sleep," she said.
"I don't want to miss anything."

But when the house was all
quiet and dark and everyone else
was asleep, Dorothy slept too.
She had small, pale dreams.

Down in her covers, deep in her bed,
she had cold, sour dreams.
"Nothing nice for me?" said Dorothy
in her dream. "Nothing nice at all?"

One dream shone a little
and Dorothy held it close.
It was only the end of
a dream, but
Dorothy thought
it was lovely.

"I'd like the rest of that. I want it all," Dorothy thought when she woke up. "I'll go to sleep early tonight so I don't miss any of it."

And so she did. That
night Dorothy went right to
sleep. She went past the cold,
sour dreams to where the
lovely dreams were waiting.
She chose the beautiful
dream she wanted.

"Tra-la-la," sang Dorothy
in her dream.

"You slept all night," said Dorothy's mother. "Are you all right?"

"Are you feeling well?" asked her father.

"You didn't sing and dance," said Dorothy's sister.

"You didn't look at books and draw pictures," said Dorothy's brother.

"But I didn't miss anything," said Dorothy. "I had a beautiful dream."